A Duck, Duck, Porcupine! Book

My Kite Is Stuck!

And Other Stories

Salina Yoon

BLOOMSBURY
NEW YORK LONDON OXFORD NEW DELHI SYDNEY

For Cameron and Bergen, with love!

First published in the United States of America in January 2017
by Bloomsbury Children's Books
www.bloomsbury.com

Bloomsbury is a registered trademark of Bloomsbury Publishing Plc

For information about permission to reproduce selections from this book, write to
Permissions, Bloomsbury Children's Books, 1385 Broadway, New York, New York 10018
Bloomsbury books may be purchased for business or promotional use. For information on bulk purchases please contact Macmillan Corporate and Premium Sales Department at specialmarkets@macmillan.com

Library of Congress Cataloging-in-Publication Data
Names: Yoon, Salina, author.
Title: My kite is stuck! and other stories / by Salina Yoon.
Description: New York : Bloomsbury Children's Books, 2017.
Summary: Loud and in-charge Big Duck, quiet and clever Little Duck, and friendly and gentle Porcupine are back in another charming trio of stories.
Identifiers: LCCN 2016025134 (print) | LCCN 2016030529 (e-book)
ISBN 978-1-61963-887-7 (hardcover) • ISBN 978-1-61963-888-4 (e-book) • ISBN 978-1-61963-889-1 (e-PDF)
Subjects: | CYAC: Ducks—Fiction. | Porcupines—Fiction. | Friendship—Fiction. | BISAC: JUVENILE FICTION / Animals / Ducks, Geese, etc. | JUVENILE FICTION / Social Issues / Friendship. | JUVENILE FICTION / Family / Siblings.
Classification: LCC PZ7.Y817 Mu 2017 (print) • LCC PZ7.Y817 (e-book) | DDC [E]—dc23
LC record available at https://lccn.loc.gov/2016025134

Art created digitally using Adobe Photoshop
Typeset in Cronos Pro
Book design by Salina Yoon and Colleen Andrews
Printed in China by Leo Paper Products, Heshan, Guangdong
1 3 5 7 9 10 8 6 4 2

All papers used by Bloomsbury Publishing, Inc., are natural, recyclable products made from wood grown in well-managed forests. The manufacturing processes conform to the environmental regulations of the country of origin.

Three Short Stories

One

My Kite Is Stuck!

Two

A New Friend

Three

Best Lemonade Stand

One

My Kite Is Stuck!

Oh no!
My kite is stuck
in the tree!

I can't fly up that high yet.

Don't worry, Big Duck.
I will knock it down
with my ball.

Kick!

Oops! My ball is
stuck in the tree.

Don’t worry,
Porcupine.
I will get it
down with
Little Duck’s
hula hoop.

I don't think
your kite,
my ball, or
Little Duck's
hula hoop
is coming
down from
the tree.

squeak
squeak

Oh, Little Duck.
That is exactly
what we need!

ONE,
TWO,
THREE . . .

THROW!
It's stuck!
Hmm.

There is just one thing left to do, Porcupine.

What's that, Big Duck?

Heave ho!

REALLY?!

Little Duck, just what we need!

We can finally play with our toys!

Two

A New Friend

I made a new friend, Big Duck!

That is not a friend,
Porcupine. That is a BUG!

It is not a bug.
It is a BEE!

A bee is not
a friend.

But Bee is MY friend!

A friend shares with you.
Can Bee share?

Bee shares
her honey!

And Bee shares
her flowers.

A friend plays with you.
Can Bee play?

Bee plays tag!

And Bee plays hide-and-seek!

I will not play
with a boring
BUG!

Duck, duck, goose—
you’re “it,” Bee!

What are you doing, Big Duck?

I am playing with my new friend!

But that is
a bug!

Yes it is—a LADYbug! Bugs are fun.

qua

Little Duck is
playing tag!

aACK!!!

I am glad Little Duck made a new friend!

Three

Best Lemonade Stand

Let's make a
lemonade stand,
Porcupine!

Okay, Big Duck!
I love lemonade.

I will paint.

I will hammer.
tap!
tap!

Lemon yellow is so lemony!

tap!
tap!
brush!
brush!

pick!
pick!

Are we ready to open our lemonade stand, Big Duck?

No, we are not ready,
Porcupine. We need . . .

. . . a SIGN! Go get your crayons, Little Duck!

Fresh Squeezed

Lemonade

Fresh Squeezed

25¢

a cup

Are we ready now?

No, we need . . .

. . . CURTAINS!

Look! Our first customers!

Lemonade!

Lemonade, please!
Uh-oh.
We forgot the LEMONADE!!
Lemonade
Fresh Squee

squeeze!
squeeze!
stir!
stir!
Sugar

clink-swish!

clink-slosh!

Lemonade
Fresh Squeezed
25¢
a cup

Best lemonade!

Mmm. The best!

This needs more ice.

This really *is* the best lemonade I ever had!

Curtains make all the difference!

Lemonade

Fresh Squeezed
25¢
a cup

sip!
sip!